# ALL ABOUT OPP...

# FRONT or BACK?

BY ADELINE ZUBEK

Gareth Stevens
PUBLISHING

first concepts

Front and back
are opposites.
This is the front
of the boy.

3

This is the back
of the boy.

This is the front
of the car.

This is the back
of the car.

This is the front
of the cat.

11

This is the back
of the cat.

13

This is the front
of the truck.

15

This is the back
of the truck.

17

This is the front
of the dinosaur.

19

This is the back
of the dinosaur.

21

Point to the front
of the bike.

23

Please visit our website, www.garethstevens.com. For a free color catalog of all our high-quality books, call toll free 1-800-542-2595 or fax 1-877-542-2596.

Cataloging-in-Publication Data

Names: Zubek, Adeline.
Title: Front or back? / Adeline Zubek.
Description: New York : Gareth Stevens Publishing, 2020. | Series: All about opposites
Identifiers: ISBN 9781538237182 (pbk.) | ISBN 9781538237205 (library bound) | ISBN 9781538237199 (6 pack)
Subjects: LCSH: English language–Synonyms and antonyms–Juvenile literature. | Facades–Juvenile literature. | Polarity–Juvenile literature.
Classification: LCC PE1591. Z82 2020 | DDC 428.1–dc23

First Edition

Published in 2020 by
**Gareth Stevens Publishing**
111 East 14th Street, Suite 349
New York, NY 10003

Designer: Sarah Liddell
Editor: Therese Shea

Photo credits: Cover, p. 1 (front) Ratikova/Shutterstock.com; cover, p. 1 (back) vubaz/Shutterstock.com; cover, p. 1 (background) Portare fortuna/Shutterstock.com; pp. 3, 5 Andrei Shumskiy/Shutterstock.com; pp. 7, 9 nitinut380/Shutterstock.com; pp. 11, 13 Dorottya Mathe/Shutterstock.com; pp. 15, 17 Robert Pernell/Shutterstock.com; pp. 19, 21 LuXpics/Shutterstock.com; p. 23 Galyna Myroniuk/Shutterstock.com.

Printed in the United States of America

CPSIA compliance information: Batch #CS19GS: For further information contact Gareth Stevens, New York, New York at 1-800-542-2595.